The Eden Book Society

100 Years of Unseen Horror

THE CASTLE

Chuck Valentine

First published in 1972
by The Eden Book Society

The Eden Book Society

First published in Great Britain in 2021 by The Eden Book Society, an imprint of Cinder House Publishing Limited.

Print ISBN 978-1-911585-50-3
Ebook ISBN 978-1-911585-51-0

Printed and bound in Great Britain by
Clays Ltd, Elcograf S.p.A

www.edenbooksociety.com

www.deadinkbooks.com

About the Society

Established in 1919, The Eden Book Society was a private publisher of horror for nearly 100 years. Presided over by the Eden family, the press passed through the generations publishing short horror novellas to a private list of subscribers. Eden books were always published under pseudonyms and, until now, have never been available to the public.

Dead Ink Books is pleased to announce that it has secured the rights to the entire Eden Book Society backlist and archives. For the first time, these books, nearly a century of unseen British horror, will be available to the public. The original authors are lost to time, but their work remains and we will be faithfully reproducing the publications by reprinting them one year at a time.

We hope that you will join us as we explore the evolving fears of British society as it moved through the 20th century and eventually entered the 21st. We begin our reproduction with 1972, a year of exciting and original horror for the Society.

Chuck Valentine

Chuck Valentine was born in Chicago in 1940 and spent much of his adult life as a botanist. After a near-fatal accident involving the deadly monkshood plant and the loss of one toe, he settled in Shrewsbury, England, and began a new career as a writer. His debut novel, *Devil's Helmet at Dawn*, was described by *Horror 108 Digest* as 'deeply disturbing'.

i)

~~Fifth draft.~~
~~It began with Dad dying.~~

I remember being shocked when I first saw white flakes falling from the sky. I was five years old at the time. My hand shook as I opened the latch of my bedroom window and spread out my palm. It felt like being licked by a cold animal. I'd thought that snow was a fairy-tale, something my father had invented for the purpose of a good story. The discovery that water vapour in the air really did convert into crystals of ice took some days for me to accept; I had dreams where I wandered white landscapes in confusion. Zombies, ghouls, vampires, hounds of hell: these were the things I thought were real, creatures woven into the shadows of the streets, lurking in the woods on my way to school, watching and waiting. Just as I discovered that snow was true, I had to learn that these were false. Growing up was a slow process of disappointment as more things turned out to be unreal than real.

I suppose the memory would have made a good anecdote for the reporter. Mum and I have been lined up by Dad's bookcases; the *flash! – flash! – flash!* of a photographer's camera sears luminous squares on my vision. You've probably seen similar pictures plastered across those glossy colour supplements. Dad's study is legendary, a mythical room that floats in the collective imagination, a mecca for would-be writers. There's a library of 2000 books lining the walls, and an old writing desk made of oak, on which Dad's Sheaffer fountain pen lies poised, a little blurt of blue ink stained on the paper underneath. On the wall hangs a print of an Egon Schiele painting, a self-portrait of his murky self and a figure behind him that lies somewhere between a shadow and a twin, an icy doppelganger. The title of the painting is *Death and Man.* The large windows look out over our back garden; when I was a kid, I always thought those tall evergreens seemed sinister, sentinels looking in as Dad's words poured onto page. He was famous for redrafting every book twenty, thirty times.

They've taken a lot of pictures of us in here over the past two years. In the early photos, the ones taken just after his death, me and my mother looked like my old jeans, frayed and stonewashed with sadness. I used to hate being dragged in for photoshoots. I refused to smile and once, hands dangling by my sides, I flicked a secret V sign which made it to the final cut. I've got used to the charade now. And I'm proud of my father, even if his success has pretty much ruined my life.

"We'll go into the living-room for questions," says Mum. She's always nervous about anyone being in his study for too long. A few months ago, a cobweb in the doorway brushed onto a reporter's shoulder. She looked as though she wanted to confiscate it and frame it.

That's when I see it – just as I'm leaving. An anomaly. I must've looked at Dad's bookshelves a thousand times; the middle case contains all 231 of his books; I've read every single one. How could I have failed to notice it? A fat volume, wedged between *The Temptress* and *The Screaming Skull of Templeton Muse*. His name, *Magnus Hunt*, is patterned on the cream spine.

There's no time to check it, for we're ushered into the living-room and it's propaganda time. Mum pours out tea, offers bourbon biscuits. The reporter refuses them.

"Magnus's titles are still selling at a rate of 500,000 a year. What do you think is the reason for their enduring appeal?"

"I think people enjoy being frightened..." Mum spouts. I've heard it all a hundred times before. Horror stories enable readers to enjoy fear, a positive stress, a catharsis that makes them feel more alive. These are words Dad once spoke in an interview. When Mum cites them, they sound like an echo of an echo.

"His last book, *The Ritual...*" the reporter checks his notes. "It focused on witchcraft, Magnus's final pre-occupation. There were rumours that you yourself had been inspired to dabble..."

I lower my face, conceal my smile. Mum combs her hair with her fingers and gives an elusive reply. The rumour was first started by one of Dad's former assistants, as a revenge for a swift dismissal: *Magnus's wife is a witch who performs spells, he doesn't even want to write about witchcraft, it's her who's dictating his work.* Mum's mortification dissipated when her friends said it gave her an aura of mystique. I'm not convinced Mum's aura could seem anything but beige. She wears old lady clothes and thinks *The Godfather* is too dark for her to see at the cinema. I can't believe that the reporter – nodding and making notes – isn't humouring her.

"And you, Jaime, you're 20 years old –"

"Nineteen," I correct him, hating the slight stutter on the 'N'.

"Do you get tired of being the son of a famous writer?"

"No." I feel heat in my cheeks. "I think my Dad's books are amazing."

I watch him write it onto his pad. I don't believe in God. I used to sneer and quote Nietzsche when my mother told me that Dad was safe and happy in heaven. She insisted that he would be in a huge library, writing more books for the angels to enjoy, having a ball. Sometimes I can't help collapsing into the sentimental, picturing him listening in on the interview, nodding and grinning.

"Famously, you had to move schools three times because you were bullied as a result of your father's fame."

He's talking about one interview, just one, where I broke down crying in the middle and Mum had to cut it short. What a bastard, bringing that up. I stutter protest and Mum cuts in:

"He's fine! He's very proud of his Dad's achievements."

She takes my hand and squeezes it and I squeeze back, and she carries the rest of the interview, with stories and soundbites and even a tear. Between our palms, a thin layer of sweat forms.

"So – I spoke to your accounts dept and they said the £30 would be transferred this afternoon?" Mum asks in a brisk voice, as the interview wraps up.

"I'll check when I get back to the office." The reporter looks vaguely disapproving.

I give him an apologetic look.

At the front door, I stand in my mother's shadow. ~~He's driving a yellow Beatle and as he drives away, I picture the car veering round the corner, the tyres losing grip, windows becoming knives, impaling his body.~~ I cry protest as Mum goes to close the door, for if I can watch him, I can keep the car steady – but she slams it shut with a frown.

In the kitchen, she puts back the unused bourbons into the biscuit tin.

"You shouldn't go on about money. It makes us seem like we're just trying to get rich off Dad."

"But how are we supposed to live? There's still a mortgage on this place." She pulls the tea bag from the reporter's mug, puts it onto a saucer to be reused later.

I point out that we get thousands of thousands in royalties every sodding year and she argues that fashions change, Dad could go out of favour overnight and I'm too young to understand how cruel life can be. I laugh at that one, and she looks meek. I storm out, about to retreat to my room, when I remember.

I open the study door very quietly, go to the shelf, remove the strange book, and head up to my bedroom with a bulge under my jumper.

It's a fat volume. The cover is cream and a little tatty. The title on the inside page says *The Castle.*

Maybe this is what Dad would call a proof copy, one of those previews for journalists. But, if so, why weren't final copies ever published? Then I see the dedication:

For Jaime.

I breathe out slowly, shakily, my eyes burning.

I need a moment. I put the book down on the bed and go over to the window. My breathing normalises. When I was a kid, I used to hate this view, dissected by fancy lattice diamonds: the rolling lawn, apple trees, the plashing fountain. I used to wish that there'd be some massive fuck up with a tax bill (Mum was always fretting about those) and that we'd end up in one of those hunched up terrace houses on the bad side of town, with black and white TVs and scrubby lawns laced with rubbish and twisty weeds.

Sometimes someone from school would come back to my house and wander about the ten odd bedrooms with awe. But then, the next day, however nice they'd been to me, they'd go back to following the herd. They'd remain silent when Laura and Rob and all those bastards started the jeers: "*Book boyy… Daddy's book… givus your Dad's signature… worth a million, isn't it, book boyyy…*"

All over now, I keep telling myself, but the poison of it is still sharp. *A fresh start,* I insist. History will not repeat. I've got my 'A' level grades – an A and two Bs. Next month I'm heading up to Scotland to study Philosophy. Mum was mostly happy for me, though once she wept, "You're going to desert me and leave me here all by myself and then what will I do?"

Usually the puff on Dad's books has certain key phrases that crop up repeatedly, like 'a tale that will give you goosebumps' or 'a book that will grab you tight and won't let you go', and always rounds off with 'a thrilling storyteller who is much loved by adults and children alike'. The blurb on *The Castle* just says:

This is a book of two halves that explores the interplay of free will and fate

Fate was something that Dad and I used to debate. Once when we were walking in the local woods, we reached a path of two forks and he said, "Which way?", and then begin to riff on all the possible consequences that might result from my decision – injury, love, robbery, death – until the weight of it felt unbearable. I said, "Let's toss a coin." Dad was unimpressed. "Never leave your destiny to fate," he lectured, "because this is *your* choice." I argued back quickly that a coin toss is always influenced by the one who tosses it, the subconscious has its say, and all that Freudian crap. And Dad said, you're still leaving a slither of that decision to fate, and who knows if the gods are smiling on you? I quoted Wittgenstein at him, that two leaves are blowing in the wind, and one says, "Let's go this way now" and the other "That way" but both are at the mercy of the wind; then I chose the second path. We reached its end with such a sensation of anti-climax that both us burst out laughing.

I open up the book. On the first page:

BOY A

Boy A is standing in the misty gloom, his hands in the pockets of his Levi jeans. The night is a chill on his skin.

He stares at the Castle; it looks like something from his childhood nightmares, turrets stark against the light of the moon. Bats fly up in a fire of black wings; he shivers with pleasurable dread.

He walks towards the Castle, until he comes to a front door made of oak. A weathered gargoyle holds an ancient knocker in its mouth.

I break off and flick through the book, discovering that the two stories intersect. *Boy A* is printed in Times New Roman on white pages; the alternative story has been printed upside-down, red font on black pages, and its beginning is the last page: *BOY B.*

Boy B is standing in the misty gloom, his hands in the pockets of his Levi jeans. The night is a chill on his skin. He stares at the Castle; it looks like something from his childhood nightmares, turrets stark against the light of the moon. He swallows and ducks at the sight of bats swooping overhead; he wants nothing more than to be home, safe in his bed.

He decides to skirt the edges of the Castle.

I wonder which boy is the protagonist and which is the doppelganger shadow. I'd probably be like *Boy B,* more coward than hero, which makes me want to follow *Boy A's* narrative, as though his strength might seep from the page. Then I consider that my father favoured plot twists, reversals; the openings might be illusory. From below, I hear Mum, calling me down for dinner.

Twilight is soft in the sky as I sit on my bed, holding *The Castle* in my hands, stroking its cover. The year after he died, I devoured nothing but the books he'd published, but over time the words became stale. I'm tempted to read more before bed, but I'm knackered and this book is fresh. Maybe I should draw it out, savour it slowly.

Sleep comes quickly. I am in the Castle. I run from room to room, and the lights go out one by one, darkness chasing after me, and I'm calling for Dad and my voice echoes around the high ceilings, spirals up into the turrets, sings out into the sky, but he never replies –

I wake up in a sweat, my cheeks damp with tears. Rolling over, I hug my pillow, sobbing into it. Over the past year, I've been telling myself that I am healing, the cut of each day a little less painful. But then the wound opens up again and I'm shocked by the sudden red spurts of memory. The hospital bed. Dad dying, not in that neat, romantic way they do in films, but slowly, his hand becoming limp in mine, his body just body, a monotonous note on a machine, a thing, a nothing. Back at school, I wanted a fight, wanted to punch and bruise, but for once everyone was kind and quiet and left me alone, which only made me feel a whole lot worse.

3.37 a.m.

I can't sleep. I reach out for the book again. I favour *Boy B* this time, anticipating a paler subplot, but outside the Castle, *B* finds himself in danger:

He hears faint noises in the distant, sees black shapes in the trees, the suggestion of something animal. And then: the sound of a woman weeping. She seems to be trapped inside the Castle.

Damsel in distress featured frequently in his stories. Whenever my Dad used to sign books, there were always more women in the queue than men. He told me that generally women tended to read more than men. They often lingered when he signed their books, put their hand on his shoulder, passed over little notes with phone numbers. He said to me, *Jaime, your Mum is a magnificent woman; she's the only one for me.*

When I see the words appearing, I sit up and adjust my lamp, figuring it's a trick of the light. They're written in a scrawl beneath the main text:

HELP ME! HELP ME! PLEASE, I'M TRAPPED HERE!

I hold it up so that the full beam of the lamp is harsh on the page and as more words materialise, I stare in shock:

OH PLEASE HELP ME, I'VE BEEN HERE SO LONG, I'll DO ANYTHING, HELP ME HELP ME HELP ME.

I snap the book shut, toss it onto the floor, pull up the covers and turn off the light. For hours, I lie rigid, not daring to move.

"What are you doing today?"

My eyes are sleepydust-clogged. My mother is in my room. She's saying something about it being past eleven and it's not healthy to sleep so late, I'll get into a bad body clock, and will I come with her into town to pick out some throws for the sofa. I groan and tell her I'm not a kid anymore, she has no right to wake me up. She sifts through the heap of dirty washing on my chair and begins to fold it up. I mumble that this is completely stupid and pointless since the washing machine will only rudely unfold them, when I heard her say, "Oh!"

"What?" I'm awake now. There's something ominous in her voice and she's bending down –

She's got hold of Dad's book. Her face clenches. "Where did you get this?"

I tell her that I found it in Dad's study.

"Well, you shouldn't have taken it. You had no right to."

"What?" Normally it's fine for me to take whatever book I like, as long as I treat it with care, use a bookmark, and put it back where I found it. "It's dedicated to me. It's mine."

"No, no, not this one. It's not one of the texts you can have," she says, as if she is a teacher and I've wandered off the syllabus.

I throw off the covers and cry, "*Mum!*" My fists are balled and the look on her face frightens me. I recoil in shame: I'd never hurt her.

Stalemate. I watch her leave with my precious book and I head for the bath. When I wander down, I find a note. *Gone to town, back in two hours,* it says. I go into Dad's study. I scour and search, but I can't see the book anywhere.

ii)

R.I.P
MAGNUS HUNT
1919-1970

There were a lot of flowers left here, the first year after he died. Jam jars with candles, notes in various languages. And then came a craze for fans to leave pens, inky ends thrust into the earth, which stick out from his grave like the quills of a hedgehog.

I kneel down. The grass is a little damp from the afternoon's shower. Closing my eyes, I whisper, "Is it you, Dad? D'you need my help?" The landscape sings around me – the birds, the wind, the trees, the traffic. A distant cry makes me jump, until I realise that it's just the sound of kids playing. I carry on whispering, but there is no reply. I feel the urge to punch the grave, dig my hands into the soil, smear mud across my face in streaks of grief. I tell myself, in a voice that sounds like my Mum's, that Dad was a taciturn man; words were his way.

The Temptress is a cottagey pub on the edge of our village. Its original name was The Goat but they took down the sign five years ago and renamed it after one of Dad's most famous books. When I walk in, there are a few doubletakes. The barman gives me a nod, and I feel anxious that he's comparing me, a square sporting a rucksack, with my father, who at closing time would be at the bar surrounded by fans, buying drinks for all, downing whiskeys, signing bare flesh, roaring laughter. I head to a table by the wall, but there's a signed photo of Dad hanging up there. I sit near the cigarette machine instead.

I open my copy of *Beyond Good and Evil.* A few tables ahead, there's a particularly dense cloud of smoke wreathed around six or seven heads. I recognise that red hair; Philippa Jenkins and I used to play together as kids. People joked we looked like brother and sister. In high school, she joined the gang of cool kids and though she never bullied me, she never made much effort to be friendly either.

I can't tell if her wave is a greeting or a piss-take. So I give her a vague sort of smile and focus on my book.

God is dead, Nietzsche declared. Back in the middle ages, the church dictated peoples' lives and everyone lived according to a set narrative. Your fate was in God's hands, the priests were in charge, and you knew that even if you were living in a horror story of bad pay and crap food, your last chapter was a guaranteed happy ending in heaven. Then science came along. God was slayed. Suddenly people lost the plot and got messed up trying to find a new one. Maybe they didn't know what to do with their own autonomy. A slave morality seeped into the masses. The priests became the nobles, vital with aristocratic freedoms; for their believers, humility and weakness became a virtue, joy deferred to heaven. This was a negation of life, felt Nietzsche. As a result, the slaves were poisoned by their *ressentiment.* (When I hear that word, I think of Mum, caged by grief, as though my Dad's death was somehow her fault.) Christians love to make us all feel guilty, he went on, because it explains our daily angst – *I am sinful, therefore I suffer*. It's a way of managing our horror in the face of meaningless suffering. But suffering is not explicable in this way; it cannot be simplified…

I don't get everything Nietzsche says, but that's okay. Everyone has their take on him, even Heidegger, who thought that Nietzsche's secret notebooks contained all his most important ideas, not his published works. When I first discovered philosophers, I treated their work like gospels, but the more I read, the more I realised each one just had their slant on life. I don't have to use the term *ghost* about Dad, or even *soul*, which is too religious and the sort of term Mum would use. But what if, what if some spark of his consciousness, some energy, quiddity has remained? After all, Dad wasn't ready for death. I remember the shock of his diagnosis. It was the first time I'd ever seen him cry. Mum sat him down on the sofa, her hand on his back, and his voice cracked like he was a little boy, as he wept that he had a dozen more books planned out and how would he ever get to write them.

In his final weeks, Mum and I took dictation from him as he lay in his rotting body. His stories became nonsensical, characters' names changing, plot twists ludicrous and oddly sadistic, as though he was an angry deity taking revenge, making them suffer worse torments than his own. When I dared to challenge him, he spat out that He was the Writer, how dare I question him, and Mum took me aside and said, he's not himself, humour him. Once, when I brought him a glass of water with a straw, his frail fingers curled into my scalp. I was afraid to pull away, of fighting back and hurting him. By the time

Mum came, there was a damp chunk of my hair in his palm. He was staring at it, muttering, *give me fire, give me fire, fire for the ritual…* It seemed he could no longer tell the difference between the world of his books and real life.

I take a big gulp of beer. The bell clangs for last orders.

I picture his spark leaving his body as he died, searching for a safe place, seeking the familiar: his study. There, he grew tired, banging against books until one yielded and became his papery womb. He may have been sleeping when I disturbed him. Or maybe he'd been screaming for help every day for two years before I found him, oh God, and –

"Hey," Philippa calls out from her table. I keep my eyes on the page.

Finally, she turns back to her gang and I feel my fingers, locked tight, loosen on *Beyond Good and Evil.* I reread the same sentence a few times, snagged by a memory. Me and Philippa, six or seven years old, sitting in the woods as I told her my nightmare. The Castle… a flit of a wing, a butterfly I forced back into its cocoon long ago, into the soup of forgetting. There was a Castle in real life. Scotland. I was five years old, or six? Six, I think. The long, long drive. Mum and Dad sitting in the front; Dad driving. He kept turning the radio on, she kept turning it off. She'd spurt out angry words and his retaliation was news bulletins at top volume. I thought I had done something to upset them and pressed my face to the window, gazing at the silhouettes of mountains against the vast, cloud-swirling sky. The next day we all visited the Castle. I remember the desk in the entrance hall, the old woman selling tickets in the gloom. A corridor of skeletons. Mum tried to take Dad's hand but he pulled away, so she held me close instead. Dad's hand was covered in little spiders, but when I cried out in horror, he knelt down and showed me that there were words scrawled onto his skin, ideas for his new book. That night our visit translated into nightmare. I woke up screaming that I was standing in the hallway of the Castle when crazed black hounds lunged up against the windows, snarling to get in. I ended up in bed between Mum and Dad.

I'm a magpie, Dad once said in an interview: I watch and I steal and I insert my jewels and gems into my books. Now, knowing that the book is a doppelganger of our history, I feel anxious. A reporter asked Dad if he felt scared when he wrote his horror novels and I was surprised when he replied, "Utterly terrified – I draw on my deepest fears. The reader isn't going to be scared if I'm not scared myself."

The second clanging of the bell. Closing-time. I wait for the rowdiest drunks to leave, then follow. Outside, I nearly trip on my shoelace and bend to tie it. Someone sings out a joke about me being a clumsy dick and I flick them a V sign.

Philippa.

Her red hair is mussed, her feline eyes bloodshot. She grabs me and I'm about to shake her off, even spit, I'm so angry that she'd take the mickey like this – when suddenly her lips are warm against mine. Her breath is in my hair. Her teeth on my neck. I am just starting to respond when her friend calls her and she laughs, strokes my cheek and says she has to go.

She attempts a few wobbly cartwheels down the lane, her laughter ghosting behind her. Am I supposed to chase after her? I look up at the half-moon, wishing it would whisper me advice. I find women inexplicable. Then I relive the kiss and a big grin stretches across my face.

It's a one mile walk home. I wander down the lanes that bisect the silent fields. Most days since Dad died have felt black and white. Now I'm lit up neon. And – this is less poetic – I've got a hard-on. I can never make choices in the present, only in the aftermath of deciding can I work out if I've got it right, and usually I feel I should have gone for *B* instead of *A*. Now I know it: I should have cartwheeled after her. I should have cartwheeled *into* her. So we both collapsed laughing on the ground and kissed again and had sex on the forest floor, leaves beneath us, the night on our skin, the trees watching.

Her kiss has bound me back into the real world. The book I discovered no longer scares me. The strange words were just a narrative trick, a joke, no more. Tomorrow I'll start packing for uni. I'll make a list of stuff to take, start hitting the second hand bookshops. I'll be alright there. There'll be beers, friends, girls like Philippa. I'll be alright.

iii)

Mum's gone out to get some milk; the milkman only left one pint today instead of the usual two. I've got about fifteen minutes to find the book. Blue, red, pristine, robust, tatty, dying – my eyes are scanning the spine of every damn book in my father's study. Upstairs, I enter their bedroom (I still can't get used to calling it her room). Those framed black and white pictures on the wall magnetise my gaze and then repel it. They depict a couple in their early twenties, smoking, messing about, making faces, kissing. I wouldn't have known they were my mother and father unless told, their skin looks so shiny, their eyes bright. This was all before Dad was famous, when Mum worked fifteen hours a day in a local bakery to make ends up meet whilst he stayed home and scribbled.

I open the chest of drawers by her bed. Paracetamols, tampons, pencils rattle around. In the next drawer I find a package the size of a book, wrapped in black cloth. I unwrap it…

The Castle.

I realise that I'm not sure if I really did want to find it. I sit there on the bed, the clock's tick taunting me, and I feel lost again, afraid to open it, afraid to put it back.

Boy A, Boy B. I reread the openings of each, flicking from front to back. I feel more certain today that *Boy A* is the narrative I want to read and favour first; I can imagine Philippa being more keen to kiss him.

Boy A bangs loudly on the Castle door. When there is no reply, he yells for someone to open up.

The door creaks open as though an invisible hand has opened it. The interior doesn't look very inviting. It is dark, gloomy and cold. It smells of sadness and lost dreams.

I turn the page.

He stands in the hallway, facing a main hall with a very high ceiling. He has a choice: he can venture into the hallway or wander down the side corridor, where a line of skeletons in rusting armour are standing.

They don't seem to be alive.

And then it happens again.

Here, in the sober daylight. There's a violence and beauty about the words as they emerge, as though clawed onto the page by a fountain pen.

HELP ME.
PLEASE GET ME OUT OF HERE.

When I wrap the book back in its cloth, it looks as though I've created a coffin around it. My hands are trembling. The cloth is rumpled, I've made a mess of it, Mum will know I've found her hiding place. I unwrap it, the cloth falls to the floor and I go to pick it up and drop the book. It falls open at page 58, at an adventure in the future of *Boy B*'s zigzagging destiny, something about a choice between two trapdoors. And the words scream out at me again:

DON'T IGNORE ME, I WON'T HARM YOU, PLEASE JUST HELP ME.

I grab a pencil from the drawer. My hand is so quivery that my writing slants all spooky too:

Who are you?
TRAPPED IN THIS BOOK.
Dad, it is you? Who are you? Dad?
HELP, I'M TRAPPED.
How can I help?
TURN TO PAGE 331.

Page 331. The last in the book.

It's blank, I write at the top.

No reply.

From below, I hear the slam of the front door. I wrap the book up, put it back in the drawer, and head downstairs.

* * *

Jenkins, P K
Jenkins, P R
Jenkins, S K

The Yellow Pages is such a dry book, a sensible book; comforting. The last few days I've lurched between euphoric and panic. Between thinking that Dad's book is a magical tome and I'm a hero who's found a literary grail and then telling myself that I've gone crazy. But maybe crazy isn't so bad. There was this psychiatrist on the TV last night called R. D. Laing and he was saying that people in asylums are basically normal and their reaction to a fucked-up world is just as it should be. After all, the world is such a mess, worse than it's ever been, with the Vietnam War, and the IRA bombing everything and half the country on strike. Mum wasn't convinced by the TV show. She screwed up her face and muttered that Laing was nuttier than his patients. So maybe I do just need therapy and Valium.

An urge has come over to me to see Philippa again. Her kiss made me feel so… normal. It grounded me, bound me back into the world, dissolved my cares.

Philippa's Mum, Penelope, used to work as Dad's assistant, many years back. Dad got through his assistants pretty fast. He was kind, but very pernickety. A spelling mistake in a letter he'd dictated in reply to a fan would cause him to tear it up. I checked his study for her number, but though there was a long list of assistants' names (15 in total), hers wasn't listed. So I dial up the first Jenkins with a P and each whir of the dial as it completes its arc is agonising.

"Hello, is Philippa there?"

Wrong number.

Three more wrong numbers. On my next attempt, as the dial swirls its fourth whir, I slam down the receiver. I pull on my coat and head into the summer twilight. By the front gate I pause, like an animal seeking a scent on the breeze. Which way, which page, which decision might lead me to accidentally bump into Philippa? I could go to The Temptress pub but it might be the last place she'll be if she's only just drunk there. Is she is a woman of habit or variety? I'd say variety. Oh God, are all these minute decisions that we make each day the work of ourselves, or are we just little puzzle pieces being lifted and moved about to fit the design, which is why only a few get the centre and the rest of us make up the boring edges? I suddenly feel so glum that I nearly turn back and figure I'll just sit in my room, reading Nietzsche, but when I look back at the house, I see the words *Help me* appearing on the page again. Maybe it's not the book that's screwing with my mind. Maybe it's home.

In The Temptress, I down a pint. And then another. The panic dilutes into a browny haze. The people around me chat and moan. Bowie is playing on the juke box. *Help me.* I go to the machine and buy some cigarettes I don't want.

The next morning, I'm heading to the library, when she shows up.

iv)

The sun is warm on my shoulders as I walk down the lane towards the library. The birds are raucous today. I still find their song eerie. When I was a kid, I believed a story my father told me that birds were Jekyll and Hyde creatures; they morphed into bats by night, then feigned soft feathers and pleasant twitter by day. I have *The Castle* in my rucksack, having stolen it from Mum's drawer. I thought it might be safer to open it in a public place.

Behind me, there's the trill of a bell. I turn and grin.

"Hey!" She peddles slowly by my side.

I say "Hey" back to her. I'm surprised by the blush on her cheeks; I thought I was the awkward one. It gives me a shot of confidence.

"How's your hangover from Thursday?" I'm nervous that she might be offended, that I'm implying she's an oafish drinker, and so her laughter tickles me.

"I had to take six paracetamol. You?"

"Oh, I never drink enough for hangovers," I say, and immediately regret it, I sound so square. "So… how were your 'A' level results?"

"Pretty bad," she says. "But who cares about that?" She trings her bell a few times.

I feel pent up because I want to tell her about my good results but she hasn't asked me like I was expecting her to. ~~Maybe she'll just ride off and as she veers across the fields a freak storm will strike the sky like a weather migraine, a flash of lightning hitting her bike and fusing them into one black charred =~~

"Hey, let's sit here." Philippa has spotted the bench under the oak by Pennington's farm.

I watch the spin of her bike wheel slow to stillness. Philippa gives me a cigarette. I'm still trying to get the hang of them and I don't want to embarrass myself with a fit of coughing, so when she holds her lighter to its tip, I feign inhaling and blow out nothing. She smiles, takes a drag, and her exhalation settles over me like smokey kiss.

I order my hands to rise up. Stroke her hair. Touch her arm. But my body remains limp, and the bees zizz in the grass, and the present grows thin. I decide to let go, because she made the first move outside the pub. Or does that mean it's my turn? This is like Dad's book. Kiss her like *Boy A* would, or chicken out like *Boy B*. Be introvert, be extrovert, be active, be passive, be a hero, be a coward –

"Your Dad is a great writer," Philippa says.

"Uh huh." I swallow. Act like *Boy A* would. Come on, do it.

"So are you going to be like him?" she asks. "Are you going to write books?"

"Oh no." I lift my cigarette and practise another un-inhale. "Me, no way! I mean, there'd be no point, cos I could never be as good as my Dad."

"What! Sure you could." She nudges me. "I remember you were always top in English."

"I did ok."

"Mr Read read out your poem about badgers."

"Everyone looked bored."

"I loved it."

"Really?" I'm sure I remember her hand clamped over her mouth, and her eyes rolling at Becky, her desk neighbour.

"I'm going to study Philosophy," I say. "I'm maybe going to teach it."

"Oh." She doesn't hide her disappointment. I look down at the spooky ash finger at the end of my cigarette, and I wish I could translate this feeling into words that would make sense. This feeling in my stomach, an endless clenching, that my whole life I will be nothing more than the son of Magnus Hunt, that his shadow will always fall over me, that I'll never find a place to bask in the light of my own achievements. Even if I did write books, even if they won prizes, even if they were better than his, everyone would say they weren't quite up to scratch. Dad was that sort of man: born to be put on a pedestal. But not many people know much about philosophy. If I spend years studying it, I'll always be one up on my students. I'll be their wise deity, dispensing answers, advising and guiding.

"Philosophy means you get to figure out what life's all about," I say. "Like Socrates said, 'The unexamined life is not worth living'."

I'm scared she'll think I'm a dick, but she looks impressed.

"I wish I could be one of your students," she says.

I feel it again: that flame of happiness. And then it trembles, in danger of flickering into nothingness, because maybe she'll get bored soon and walk off and I can't think of what to say next and I open my bag, grab the book and pull it out.

"Look," I say in a shaky voice. "Look what I found."

She stubs out her ciggie and turns it over in her hands. I boast that it's my father's final work before he died.

"Wow!" she gasps, flicking through. "This is... *different*... two boys... living out alternate narratives..."

I pass her my cigarette to hold and take the book back.

"You know what's spooky? I was using the book yesterday and I don't know, maybe I annoyed it –"

"Annoyed it? It's a book," she chuckles.

"Yes – but there was – there was..." I wish I'd never brought this up. She's going to laugh; she's going to sneer; and we won't kiss again.

"Go on," she cries, her nudge sharp now. "Tell me tell me tell me."

"This writing appeared," I say. "It just – appeared. I know it sounds stupid and maybe I was still trapped in my nightmare, but I swear that's what happened. Look."

I'm pleased when her face grows sober.

"But it's just some trick." She's forgotten the cigarette she's holding is mine and now she's sucking on it hard. "You know, like a lemon juice trick."

"What?"

"Didn't you do that when you were a kid? Squeeze juice onto a page and the invisible lettering shows up. I can't remember the science behind it, fuck it."

"But I didn't have a lemon to hand." I frown. "It just appeared, I swear, I did nothing to the book."

"Yeah, but it's something else. Like the pages have been hit by oxygen and some chemical shit's happened. Your Dad must have set it up to spook readers. It's a pretty fine trick. I do like this experimental two-boy story thing. Do the two boys ever meet in the book?"

"I've not reached that point yet. I don't know."

"Maybe they'll kill each other if they do."

She pulls out another a cigarette packet and extracts a stick of lipstick. Without a mirror, the pink is jaggedy on her lip-line. She asks me to wipe off the smudges. Then she asks if she can put the lipstick on me, so I'll look cool and glam rock. I say no, and she lunges at me and I feel bullied –

Then we're kissing again.

In my fantasises, I've been on fire with every imagined kiss. In the here and now, I find myself staring at the contours of her cheeks. I note a zit, a freckle. The book has slipped onto the bench, its hard edge teething my thigh. I shouldn't have shared it with her. My secret feels diluted; I've betrayed Dad. In the distant bushes, his face blends with the leaves, eyes like acorns, watching us with a frown.

Philippa takes my hand and puts it in her hair. It stays limp. She gets up and climbs onto her bike, red-faced. The *tings* of her bell as she rides off sound like exclamation marks.

v)

I hear Mum's key in the door and I jump up. In the kitchen, she unpacks paper bags from the grocers. She asks me why I added a lemon to her list. I tell her that I've read drinking warm water laced with lemon is healthy, resentment flickering inside me – why does she want to know everything all the time? I grab the lemon, toss it up into the air and catch it, toss and catch, toss and catch.

"I'm going to send the book back to the British Library today," she says, putting a cauliflower into the fridge.

The lemon – falling from a height – bounces off my hand, hits the kitchen floor.

"Oh, right." I swallow and pick it up. "Why there?"

"It's of historical significance." She says, sounding rehearsed. "I'll send it this afternoon."

I think of the book, still in my rucksack since yesterday.

She hasn't realised that the book wrapped in cloth in her drawer is actually a Jackie Collins. I have maybe a few hours left.

"I think Dad would have hated you to send his book there," I say, fingering a soft patch on the lemon's skin, where a bruise is forming. "I think he would have felt betrayed."

Mum makes a noise, folds up the paper bags.

As I leave the kitchen, she calls after me that lunch will be ready in an hour and she'll make my favourite, cauliflower cheese.

Upstairs in my room, I jam a chair against the door. I open the book and turn to page 331. Then I realise that I don't have a knife for the lemon.

A pen – that will do. I rummage through my drawers, finding the fountain pen that my Dad gave me for a birthday two years ago, carefully removing the packaging. When its tip hits the lemon skin, juice and ink spurt and mingle, blue and black and yellow on my fingers, flecks on my chin. I guide its dripping onto the blank page. The letters show up:

TO ENTER, YOU MUST:

- TAKE A LOCK OF YOUR HAIR.
- INSERT IT INTO A FLAME
- RECITE THE INCANTATION BELOW
- SURRENDER

Lunch tastes bland; there's too much cauli and not enough cheese. We eat in silence. Then I head back to my room.

I've got a snip of hair in one hand, my lighter flame in the other. A memory clouds my concentration: the white scab left on my scalp after Dad pulled out a fistful of my hair on his sickbed. It was the size of a one pence coin. The week he died, I kept reaching up to touch it. I hoped the scar might stay there forever but hair began to bristle and grow, like grass on the earth of a coffin. I bring the flame to the hair-lock. It makes a hiss as it fizzles its edges. As I mutter the incantation, I suffer the urge to laugh hysterically.

The stench of burning hair sobers me. The flame flares up fiery blue as it eats through the strands and my finger howls with a sear of pain –

I can hear screaming. I'm scarlet-sick, fever crawling over my skin.

My body crumples away from me like a suit of
old clothes and
I am becoming
air
then wind
it's like one of those dreams in
the dead of night when you're
flying high over skies –

but
either my body pulls me back, or my shellshocked soul flies into retreat, for I am wrenched backwards –

In my room. Safe. Solid, in a hot body. Pain in my palm. I feel out of joint, as though I've re-entered my body upside down. Black dots haze around the corners of my vision, the wallpaper ripples, its pattern melts and drips. The hair, half-charred, still lies on my palm. Around its edges is a red-burn scar. I hold out the remains of the hair, take the lighter to it, firing up the flame, *come Jaime, come on, go all the way, all the way… Is this what it was like for Dad when he died?* Slipping in and out, trapped in the physical one minute, free the next, torn between Mum and I wanting to hold him here forever, and the ache for release from his wrecked body? Flick! The lighter flares and I cry, Dad, I'm doing this for you, I'm coming to be with you, I can withstand any pain for you – but

Nothing can quite prepare me for this burning

Burning

Red and air and fire and ice…

Slam crash pain.

I feel small and very cold. It's dark. The grief in my heart is raw as the day my father died. I uncurl my palms. My lifeline is missing; my love-line looks faint. I want my true body back, I want my skin, I want the brutality of that burning scar.

The mist swirls and I feel the damp seeping through my jeans. My trainers have made an indent in the gravel. One of my shoelaces is undone.

A distant noise, like a shrieking bird. I can still hear the echo of my screams.

I force myself to stand. The Castle is there, in the distance, gothic against the streaky sky. My heart thrills with the thought: he's in there.

I'm shivering, my skin pitted with goosebumps, but I still can't move. I reach inside my pocket and find a train ticket. It's a dirty white and crumples serrate the red British rail logo. The mundane everydayness of it reassures me. I think: I'll soon be back on a train and I'll look back at this moment and I'll know it was all a crazy hallucination. I'll tell Philippa and she'll laugh and kiss me.

"You can be Boy A or Boy B." It's Dad's voice, a sound I haven't heard for years. *"You can either go to the Castle, or you can walk around it."*

"Dad?" I look up at the night sky, the furl of clouds.

No reply.

I stand there, aching for the voice again, eager to locate it. The wind swirls through the trees and the clouds flow across of the moon and the cold is becoming brutal, when it comes again:

"You can be Boy A or Boy B. You can either go to the Castle, or you can walk away."

One minute it sounds as though it's coming from the left, the next from the right. It leaves no echo. I pictured him pressing up against the membrane of the story, desperate to connect.

"Dad?"

Boy A, Boy B: a coin-toss in my mind, a forked path. As I announce that I will play *A*, I hear the doubt in my voice and repeat it with conviction. My feet crunch over the gravel and I pass a cluster of evergreens, brushed my fingers against their prickly tips. They're clearly based on the ones that overshadow Dad's study in real life; they have the look of trees that watch and listen and betray you. I'm walking through Dad's psyche, through a landscape of his imagination, and the thought disturbs and consoles me, making me feel close to him and fearful of what I might discover.

The Castle is the Scottish nightmare of my childhood, the place we visited as a family. It has an imposing, bullying air. Bats swoop about its turrets; as I approach the door, a rat scuttles away. The door looks as though it's carved from a wood native to Hell, it's so dark and dank. There's a knocker hanging in the mouth of a weather-beaten, geriatric gargoyle. Its weight is heavy in my hands. I let it fall and with its clanging bang, the frightened bats fly up in a black flame. There is a click, a creak, and then the door swings open.

My father narrates:

"Boy A enters the Castle and walks into the hallway…"

"DAD?" I call into the hallway. "DAD? ARE YOU IN THERE?"

Dad…

Dad…

Dad…

The hallway sings back to me.

I step inside. Part of me wants to laugh, it's such a generic haunted house. Ahead of me is a grand hallway, with a black marble staircase that leads up a gallery of rooms, wreathed in gloom. To my left is a corridor lit by the sickly glow of candle-lamps. Suits of armour with skeletal heads and hands poking out of their rusty parts line the walls. To my right is another corridor, the walls covered in paintings, a syrup of cobwebs obscuring my path.

I want to run through this house and call his name again and again until his real voice breaks through and I find him. Imagine, imagine taking him back with me, being back in the world, playing cricket in the garden, going for a walk in the fields, discussing his new ideas together –

"HELP ME!"

Help me…

Help me…

Me….

My heartbeat is still violent when the voice sounds again and I am shocked.

It is a female voice.

"Boy A decides that he must seek out the damsel in distress and offer his help."

I swallow, looking into the dark.

"Did I choose the right boy?" I ask.

Silence. Then, a sound of dripping, a faint creak as though a distant door is opening and closing. A spider hurries across a web.

What if she's a trap? A siren to distract me from Dad? I don't understand it. Dad's voice is so dry and cool and hers is so clawing and desperate. Perhaps this is a test where he wants me to prove I can be a hero? Perhaps by following *Boy A*'s predetermined choices, I can become him.

"Right," I say, opting for the right corridor, because paintings are less scary than skeletons.

I pick up a bent sword from a casket by the wall to slash the cobwebs down. Spiders scuttle around my feet and I play fancy-footwork, screeching disgust. The carpet is moth-eaten and they disappear into the gaps between the stone flags.

Each painting on the wall is framed by long, ragged velvet curtains. I'd imagined old men in oils, with warts and double chins. These are black and white affairs, with the eerie, experimental tone of Schiele's paintings. Each one depicts a couple making love, contorted into different shapes, their bodies made murky by thick brushstrokes, their mouths warped into Os as though they might be having orgasms, or maybe they're just screaming. The energy of each picture becomes more and more violent as they progress, until the final one makes me gasp. Up until now, I've tried to adopt an ironic detachment, but I realise the house is getting to me, sucking me in, despite its clichés. *An illusion,* I tell myself. *This is just an illusion.* My real body is back in my bedroom, lying on my bed, clutching an inky lemon. Mum will be banging on the door. My heart pinches. I hope she's not too worried.

At the end of the corridor are two long velvet curtains.

I hear the voice cry,

"HELP ME!" and I say, "Oh God," as she cries another, "HELP ME!"

And in the fading echo of her plea, my father's voice tells me that *Boy A proceeds forward to help her.* As I open the curtains, my eyes are irked by a snowfall of dust. I brush it away from my clothes and note the rusty knob: a door. So this is where the damsel is being kept.

Stone steps. They head down into a basement. I force my body on, one by one, towards a murky, flickering light. At the bottom step, I discover a single candle in a holder and I pick it up, the wax forming a crust on my skin.

A room full of oblong boxes. The *"Help me!"s* are coming from the box in the middle. I venture forward and the light and shadow from the flame spills chiaroscuro onto the inscription. It's then that I realise I am in a room of coffins.

"Hello?" I ask.

Her response to my voice is so vehement that I stumble backwards.

Then my Dad's voice interjects:

"Boy A hears terrifying screams and banging coming from the coffin.

Who could be inside – a banshee? A vampire? Or a damsel in distress?

He decides to open the coffin."

~~Pandora's Box, I think.~~ I stand and stare as the voice becomes hoarse and thins into sobbing. I don't understand this, I say to Dad silently. I thought I was going to free you. Did you just send me here to save her? I think of my father's policy of answering every single fan letter that he ever received, how he once saw a TV show where a girl was dying of leukaemia and made an anonymous donation to her family. He's sent me on this mission to do his good work. This is *his* book. Surely nothing in it can really harm me.

Even as I lift the coffin lid, I still don't believe there really is a damsel. This is a game; I know Dad's inside.

Something jumps out screaming. It clings to me and I try to yank away; it holds on tight. Then I realise it's a someone. She's weeping into my chest, begging me to help her climb out. Her legs are unsteady. Her hands scurry over her hair, removing cobwebs, shaking away dust. I step backwards away from her.

I sit on the floor, the candle set down beside me. The grief hits me again: the loss of him, the absence. I bury my face in my hands and my palms become wet.

Gradually, my body stops shaking. Through the slits in my fingers, I notice how beautiful the woman is. She's old, in her thirties. She doesn't look like a witch or a banshee; more like a princess, with her hair spun gold. An everyday princess, in jeans and a black rollneck. Is she real, or part of Dad's imagination? How could she have got hold of one of his books? She must be part of the story. A test from Dad. Maybe I will only meet him if I deserve to. Isn't that how narratives work?

I stand up. She looks me up and down, as though this is her story and I'm the sub-plot.

"Are you going to fucking help me? Because I'd rather you just killed me if this is all part of the fucking game."

I flinch, shocked.

"I heard you crying out so I entered the book. I'm here to help."

A smile breaks out across her face.

"You know how to get out of here? How did you enter?"

"Well, I was in my room and I had the book and I did the ritual." I swap the candle to my other hand, for the wax has formed a mould around my knuckles.

"The ritual? What's that?"

"What – so you didn't get in by… But how did you get in?"

"So you're his *son?*"

"I thought Dad would be in the book when I heard the screams. Is he here, have you seen him?"

"Well, it's kind of hard to escape him. He's fucking omniscient, isn't he? He's everywhere. This is all his creation, made in seven days."

"But… I thought he was trapped…"

"You're the son of God, sent to save my soul."

I lift the candle, the swelling in my chest subsiding when I see the look in her eyes.

"I'm grateful," she says, in a meeker voice. "Seriously – I am. I've been here a long time and I want to get out and –" she is fighting tears now, swallowing hard. "It's just – it's good that you came –"

"Boy A can hear something in the distance," Dad's voice interrupts us, and she clamps her hands over her ears. "*He had been wondering whether to search for a trapdoor which would lead him deeper into the Castle's foundations, but the sound makes him uneasy…"*

"There are rats down below," she says. "It's better upstairs."

I reach out and take her hand and reassure her: "Good. We'll go upstairs then. I'll make sure I get you out of here." And as we start to climb the stone steps, the echo of my footsteps echoed by hers, I swear Dad is looking down over us, nodding and smiling.

Up in the hallway, she pauses to look at the black and white oil paintings. I try to pull her away, wondering if the pictures are cursed, for they seem to steal the colour from her skin. She shakes me off irritably, moving closer and closer to the one where the woman's mouth is wide with orgasm, until the O of her mouth is same size as the O on the canvas. I think of *The Mirroring,* the novel Dad wrote about the haunted house that reflected those who entered it. It imbibed their scents, digested their reactions, conjured scenarios that would create the most concentrated horror. At the end of the book, the group were all driven mad. I tug at her again and this time she follows me, letting me lead her down the hallway, past the heaps of cobwebs, down the stone steps towards the main door. I don't remember this: a big rusty bolt. I don't remember sliding it across and locking us in. Its rust flakes orangey on my fingers. Her breath is warm on my neck as I tug and tug harder –

"Let me do it."

"But you won't be able –" I step backwards, feeling deflated. The tips of her fingers are scabbed, nails wrecked, from banging on the coffin.

"Let's both try," I say.

I shove and she yanks and the bolt moves maybe a millimetre and our faces are pink and our arms hurting with the exertion and –

"It's no good, it's a fucking *waste of time,*" she screams, and collapses against the door. "YOU BASTARD!" She kicks and punches the door.

I put my hand on her shoulder. She flinches.

"We nearly did it, the bolt was moving."

"Don't be stupid," she mutters.

"There must be other ways out," I say, but I wonder: how long has she been in here? Then: maybe she's just been here too long, like a fly hitting a window. I feel a presence behind me, like a knuckle against my shoulder blades. I look up and see two gargoyles with bulbous eyes and gloomy faces. I say a silent prayer: *Dad, can you help us? This is my fault? Should I have chosen Boy B?*

Silence.

"We should try another exit," I say, sounding more confident than I feel.

We cross the main hallway and then Dad's voice comes:

"Boy A is starting to lose his confidence. The house is beginning to get him to him. He is tempted to go upstairs, but fears deeper, darker horrors, so instead he opts for the dining-room."

"Dad?" I call again. "Dad?"

She's shaking her head at me, and I blush.

"We'll go into the dining-room," I assert.

There are tapestries on the walls of the dining-room, their cloth faded and moth-eaten. Candelabra squat on the table, little brides in cobwebbed dresses. There are about a dozen chairs with golden bowed legs lined around it, as though it's set for a tea party of ghosts. I reach for one of the chairs and approach the window. Will the glass fracture, spray at me? I glance at the woman and think: I don't even know her name. When we get out of here, I'll have to ask. I picture us embracing as we taste freedom; her whispering the reply into my ear, her breath a caress. I lift the chair and take aim –

"NO!"

"What?"

"It won't work, I've tried this, it just sets off the dogs."

Dogs? I shiver. Another detail from my childhood nightmare that Dad has woven in.

"I can fight off a few dogs," I declare, feeding off her fear, feeling strong in opposition. I can be *Boy A*, she'll see. I strike it against the window and she shouts at me again. Cracks zigzag across the glass. In the distance, they take shape, breaking out of the darkness, the silhouettes with barking jaws. I ought to draw back but I lift the chair and smash it even harder. Anger pumps through me. *You won't let me die, Dad, will you? You wouldn't let that happen? If you exist, you'll make sure they don't get me.* There's a moment where the glass – separated into fragments and diamonds – remains intact, before it dies into shatters that hit the floor and bounce off my feet and I leap backwards. Cold air pours in. The hounds are coming closer, closer, their barks forming plumes in the freezing air.

"I told you not to fucking do that!" she sobs.

"I can't believe Dad would really put us in serious danger..." I say, backing up.

One of the hounds has reached the window now. Teeth; saliva; wild black eyes.

"Run!" I grab her hand and we spin out into the hallway and Dad's voice is overhead, telling us that Boy A is feeling more terrified than he's ever felt in his life, and I say UPSTAIRS, but she says, LIBRARY, insists it's safe, it's safe, and its door is a faux bookcase, like something out of a spy film, and she punches the button for entry and we're in.

vi)

The library is identical to Dad's study at home – save for the candle-lamps flickering on the walls. The woman's breath is hissing in-out-in-out in gasps. I look up at the ceiling, wanting to hear Dad's voice, narrowing the situation down, telling me what *Boy A* would do next.

"Close," she points. "Close the curtains – they – the dogs can see –"

I hurry to the window and sweep the purple velvet curtains across.

Then I say: "Sit down."

It makes me feel very manly and authoritative to guide her over to the armchair. I hover, monitoring her, half-afraid her skin might split and crack and creepy-crawlies seep out, like the girl in *The Citadel* who offends the Insect King. Her breathing slows. She spreads open her fingers into taut stars.

"Panic attack," she explains. "I don't like dogs."

"I think they've gone now," I say, but the house responds with a pounding on the door. I picture the dogs flying up against the oak, trying to crash though. She shudders.

I reach out to rub her shoulder but at the last minute, I pull away and shove my hands in my pockets. Every detail of the study is identical to home: the line of bookcases, the middle showcasing all 231 volumes of Dad's works; another two bookcases filled with tomes that inspired him. When I see the doppelgänger book, my heart stops. Cream cover; a blurb on the back: **This is a book of two halves that explores the interplay of free will and fate.** But when I open it up, aside from *The Castle* on the title page, the pages are blank.

There's a desk by the window, some papers are scattered over it. I shuffle through them. The handwriting is different from Dad's: *I'm going to go to the coffin and lie down in it and hope I just die. That's what he wants, I think. My surrender, my suicide. He always spoke about abandonment as a state of–*

"They're mine." She's jumped up from her chair. Gathering the papers together, she stuffs them into a drawer.

"Sorry." My hands dangle by my sides, my sleeves hang loose. I don't feel in charge anymore, but awkward, like I did around Philippa.

"I've been in this place a long while," she says.

If I asked her if she was real, would she be capable of an honest answer? In sci-fi novels, the robots never believe they are created by humans; they delude themselves into thinking they've come from nature, from divine origins. Dad used to laugh about this and say they viewed *homo sapiens* as inferior gods, but I was never quite sure what he meant by this.

"I'm Jaime. What's your name?" I hold out my hand to shake hers, feeling it's the grown up, polite thing to do.

Her arms remain crossed.

"I'm Gina," she mutters.

"The same as…" I tell her that she has the same name as a girl I know, but I'm really thinking of the heroine of *The Temptress.*

I pick up *The Castle* doppelgänger.

"I thought there might be another ritual in here, but it's all blank."

"So what does this ritual involve?"

"Um, having to burn a lock of hair and then recite some words."

"Oh, sure." She raises an eyebrow.

"Really, I swear it's how I came here. It was in the book."

"It's childish. It doesn't sound like the sort of thing your Dad would put in a book."

"It's exactly the sort of thing he put in. Look, before he died, he wrote a book called *The Ritual* and did a load of research into witchcraft."

"Oh. Well, I haven't been around to read his final works of genius."

"I don't even know if he performed a ritual himself –" I swallow, afraid the theory will sound stupid. "Maybe before he died, he was afraid and he performed it to avoid the final… end…"

Gina raises an eyebrow.

"You're… you're not real, are you?" she says.

"I'm real! I'm his son! You're the figment of imagination!" My cheeks grow hot.

"I was Magnus's assistant," she asserts.

"Oh." Maybe she was one of the early ones. "I don't recognise you," I challenge her.

She laughs. "Your father had over a hundred assistants."

"He had fifteen," I say. "So… if you didn't perform the ritual, how did you get in here?"

"It was… my prison sentence."

What does she mean by that? She sits down in the armchair again, looking tired. I wonder if she wasn't a very good secretary and skewed his dictation with typos.

"When I got a job working for your Dad, I was so proud. My husband, he'd been working at the steelworks and he got laid off. We had a baby, my boy. I didn't have much experience of secretarial work and when I came to the interview – I was sitting in this very room – well, in the real world – and I was facing his desk, and I'd worn this suit that was a size too small and I wanted it so badly. I messed the interview up, but he still gave it to me."

I feel tears pressing against my eyes again, but I blink them away.

"He was working on a new book idea – exploring a horror story told by two boys, one who acts like a hero, one who acts like a human. He called them *Boy A*, *Boy B*, placeholder names, then decided not to properly name them."

"But who was the supposed to be the right boy? Which boy were you supposed to follow?"

"Neither." She shrugs. "Both. The reader has to figure that out. There's no easy ending for either of them. I ended up writing quite a bit of the book for him. It's not as though your Dad was the best prose stylist – he was all about ideas."

"That doesn't sound like Dad," I object. I feel disappointed that Gina's turning out to be just like all the others. Like Mum used to say, they were often more focused on what they could get out of Dad than what they could give, intoxicated by *ressentiment.*

Her eyes are fixed on me; her expression changes. She pats the chair next to hers, tells me to sit down. I obey her. When we're this close together, I'm conscious of her beauty again, even if her skin is streaked with dirt. Her eyes are luminous, her lips like ripe fruit.

"What I meant to say was," she says, "that sometimes he wrote very fast, so fast he could hardly get the words down, so I helped – helped facilitate that process. And your Dad asked me to brainstorm some ideas for the horror features of this book. The skeletons in the hallway – they were my idea. Ironically, I created those bloody dogs. They're my babies. Your Dad said it was important to draw on our own fears, in order to make it authentic. Well, I've been afraid of dogs ever since I was a kid, and I got bitten by a German shepherd, and so I created this hell – can you believe it? I still get panic attacks every time they come through those windows."

"Dad had an amazing imagination," I reply, frowning. I wonder whether to correct her and explain that the dogs were the materialisation of *my* nightmares, *my* fears, but she seems so fragile, I decide to keep quiet for now.

"Your father…" her voice grows pale. "I was doing a good job but – he fired me."

"It… he just got cross sometimes, and lost his temper, and did things he regretted… It must have been a long time ago," I say.

"It was. It feels like decades. After I was fired and the years were going by, and I felt so tired… Dan – my husband – he was in and out of work, and our Gabriel – my boy – I was sometimes having to skip meals so he'd be fed. I went back to your Dad and I begged him to let me come back. Of course, he'd moved on by then, had gone through several more assistants… and that's when it happened. That's how I got here."

"What d'you mean?"

"I just remember – he was angry, and he was shaking the book at me, *The Castle*. I was telling him that, if he published it, I ought to get royalties. I'd put in my contribution. He was going to profit from my phobia of dogs. And then – there was this blackness. Maybe he performed the ritual on me… I don't know… I just woke up here."

Silence.

"I'm sure he meant to let you out," I say. I can hear the trembling in my voice.

"Well, he got sick, didn't he?" she says, in a gentler tone. "He got ill and he..."

"I'm here now," I say. "I'm doing my Dad's work. I heard your screams and that's why I came. Dad must have wanted me to help you."

Gina holds my gaze, her eyes liquid, and then she reaches out and strokes my cheek.

"Do – do – you – you –" my cheek still burns from her touch. "Do you think we *can* get out? I thought... I thought I was here to save you, I thought it would be easy – I mean, a bit of a test, because if stories are too easy, that's boring, but I thought we'd get out. But – are we stuck here?"

"There must be a way. I've been stuck here so long, I've lost sight of all the possibilities. But you – I believe that you're my hero. You're going to find a way, you're the One who's been sent to solve this – this story."

I swallow, and smile shakily.

"But how long have you been here? *Years?*"

"A few years, yes."

That doesn't quite make sense. Dad only died a few

years ago, and if she saw him before he was ill, that would have been four, five years. I think she's lost track of time, the months have blurred into one long hell.

"Do we – need to – eat? Sleep?"

"We don't need to. It's good to, out of habit. I sleep, because I lose eight hours of each day that way. But you can't stay in any one room in this place too long, because he… it's a house which makes you move from one fucking horror story to the next."

"But up there – in the real world…" I wonder why I think of us being down here, when we might be above, or alongside, or inside. My sense of perspective reels; dizziness seesaws my mind. "Our bodies – what happens to them?"

"I figure we're in a coma," she says. "Our bodies are intact, but we're not present. We're joined to them by some sort of umbilical cord. We're in a liminal space."

Mum. Once, after I'd had an accident at footie practise, I went to hospital in an ambulance. I remember her running into the ward, her face raw with weeping. She's lost Dad and now me. She'll be sitting by my side in hospital, trying to wake me up, reading me a newspaper, most probably the boring bits. I feel the urge to jump up, leave Gina, and find my own way out. There's something about being with her that makes me feel murky, slowed down, as though I'm under water.

Then I feel her warm hand on mine. I look up and her eyes hold mine.

"We've both got people waiting for us."

"We should go upstairs," I say. I feel certain that this is what *Boy A* would do. "There might be an escape up there." I tug her hand, but she pulls me back down.

"We can't act until we hear your Dad giving instructions. The locks don't open until – until his voice unlocks them with the next bit of plot. The dogs – they take hours to go. We'll have to wait, sleep it out. In the morning, they'll be gone."

"What if we changed to *Boy B*, to his story?"

"You can't change halfway through, you have to follow the story through. Besides, the dogs are there in both stories, I'm afraid. Believe me, I've tried that one."

"Can we die in this book? And… what would happen in the real world if one of us did?"

"I've stayed alive, but I've not taken any risks," she says. "I follow the narrative. Or… maybe he's let me live. He could let us out any time, I reckon. He's watching us, I swear." Her words break up, become jagged, and her panic attack starts up again. I hold her hand, stroke her hair, until she calms. I tell her that my dear Dad would never hurt us. She slumps with exhaustion and her eyes close and sleep pulls her under. I crave Dad's voice, the next stage of the plot. It would give us a sense of structure, direction; it feels as though time is unravelling in here.

I get up and scour the bookshelves. This is always my routine at home before going to bed: wandering about Dad's study, sitting in his chair, reading one of his books. I attempt the opening lines of *The Haunted Kestrel,* but my eyes burn with acid tiredness. When I close them, I try to expand my consciousness, connect with the me in the real world, and I strain to catch the beep of a machine, hear Mum's voice. But – nothing. Then I consider that Gina's theory is just a theory. Being here would have driven her crazy if she didn't create some sort of myth that explained how it works. For all we know, the bodies we've left behind might be active doppelgängers who are currently eating, chatting, sleeping. How would it function? As a pastel version of me, someone who doesn't seem quite there? *You're not real, are you?* Gina taunted me. But I am real, this is the true me, even if – when I gaze down and stare at my palm I encounter the absence of my lifeline again.

I put *The Haunted Kestrel* back and exchange it for *The Temptress.*

She was in possession of a dangerous beauty, with locks that flowed over her shoulders like dying sunlight, and blue eyes that sparkled with cunning. A hero would have to be strong to resist such a temptation…

My eyes travel over to Gina, asleep on her chair. Her beauty fills me with ache. It makes me feel shrunken too, small and stupid, as though I'll never be good enough to deserve someone like her. I think of those pictures in the hallway, the black and white swirls of sex and death, and the realisation comes to me: the woman in those paintings looks like Gina. I don't understand what this means, but the revelation makes me want to jump up, run down the corridor, and examine every tiny brushstroke. At the door, however, I remember the dogs, and Gina's phobia, and her warning about the locks, and I step back. My hands curl into fists. I feel like I want to punch them against the wood until they bleed.

I turn and lay down on the floor by her feet, hungry for the forgetful dark of sleep.

vii)

I wipe sleepydust from my eyes. My sleep was fractured by nightmares; their aftermath has soiled me. There were dreams within dreams, like a series of Babushka dolls, where I suffered the illusion of false waking. In one I got up and pulled out one of Dad's books from the case and found it full of blank pages, and then another, and another, certain that if I yanked them all out, I'd find Dad behind the cases, and as they thwacked and thudded around me, I yelled his name. All the books were blank inside. In another dream, I walked down the hallway of paintings, and then – I can't remember the details of the terrible thing that happened – just the recollection of a grey fog of sound and fury. In the third, I was sitting in a theatre with Mum and Dad, watching myself on a stage, performing mime against an invisible wall. My consciousness flitted back and forth between the two selves like one of those holographic cards you can tilt this way, that way, to see an image buried in an image. I must have cried out in my sleep, because Gina woke up and slipped down onto the floor beside me. She pulled me close, my cheek in her breasts, her warm breath like a lullaby as we slipped back into sleep.

A sickly light is seeping through the curtains, highlighting her face. She looks tired, her forehead knitted in frown. I get up and open the curtains. The sky looks as though morning twilight has failed to evolve into day.

I am hungry for my father's voice, for the reassurance of being told what to do; but the waiting is driving me crazy. I try the door. It's locked, just as Gina warned. We're in that gap between chapters; we're blank page.

"We could try the ritual," I say, "but it probably won't work, as it was a ceremony to get me into the book, not out. How does it end for *Boy A*, or *B*? You must have done this a hundred times?"

"That's the cruelty of this place – I can't remember."

"What? Really? Even after all this time?"

"It's the trick of the house. You finish the story and lose the memory and then you go through again, and believe me, the déjà vu gets stronger every fucking time, and that's also part of how you become anaesthetised.

That's where you can save us. I'm so tired, so bored, I can't see any way out now, I'm numb to everything. This is your first time here, you have a completely new perspective, you can spot that anomaly, that detail which will be the clue to us escaping."

I smile and take her hand. Around us, the house shifts and creaks and groans. And my father's voice sings out above, instructing us that *Boy A* leaves the library.

The main hallway is dim. The dogs have left us. The library felt like a sanctuary but here the gloom seeps into me, greying my mind. The marble staircase before us is lined with flickering candles.

From above, Dad says:

"Boy A decides that he must be proactive. He must take action. He will climb the stairs and venture in the unknown, for danger is his compulsion; he is a boy of courage."

I'm starting to hate the monotony of my father's voice. This is his public voice, one reserved for readings, clearly enunciated, but beneath the entertaining pitch is a monotone. I want his laughter, his low, sarcastic tone, his cajoling, his shouting.

I look at her; she looks away. A new memory fragment, from last night's mares: we were standing hand in hand, looking at the paintings. They lost detail, morphed into simple sketches, as though the oils were thick layers of hatred that had distorted something once innocent.

"What if we disobey him?" I ask.

"The narrative freezes up. It's far worse. We have to obey, we have no free will here, it's all his divine plan."

"Okay, then. The stairs," I hear myself say.

She lets me guide her to the foot of the staircase. Then she presses against me, becomes my shadow.

"I'm scared," she whispers. "It's… I can't remember… but I know something bad happens up there."

"Let's be brave. Dad used to say that plots need to be in three acts and there's always a descent into the very worst point before it all comes good."

We climb the grand staircase. Halfway, it splits into two, one arching up to the left, the other to the right, both connecting to the upstairs gallery. I wait for Dad to give us another order, but the white fog drifts around us, and we wait a little longer, and a little longer, and there is nothing. We climb the left set of steps. It's hard to see clearly, but it seems that we're in a quartet of corridors that look down over the main hall. There is a chorus of doors that might lead to more rooms. The fog starts to thicken, acquires substance and swirl. My palms become damp and I realise I'm no longer holding Gina's hand. I turn to find her – when I hear a voice. It's very distant, like a crackling dialogue from a radio in one of the rooms. Someone is calling my name. Dad? I paw through the fog. *Jaime, Jaime.* It is Dad: he's here. He's here.

I should find Gina. I picture her panicking in the fog, crashing over the railings, her body a broken ragdoll in the grand hall below. But I can't stop, I want Dad, I want him all to myself. Is this a door? I fumble, find a handle. The fog churns around me. I open it up. A room with bed after bed. No – the walls are mirrored, turning the single bed into multiples. *Jaime, Jaime,* my Dad calls and I cry, *Dad, Dad, I'm here.* I run to the window. Trees and the path and no sign of Dad. I try to open the lattice window, battle with a rusty catch. *Dad. JAIME,* he says, right in my ear. I jump and turn and –

Mum is standing in the doorway. She's wearing a wedding dress with a ragged train, tears streaky on her cheeks. In one hand, she holds a shrivelled lemon; the other is busy pulling out locks of her hair. She stares down at the sprays of hair in her palm, weeping *Why won't it work, why won't the ritual work.* I tell her it did work, she made it here, now we'll be able to escape, Mum always knows what to do. But when I try to touch her, my body bangs against an invisible resistance, like a pane of glass, and I can only splay my palms against it like a mime artist. I am just inches from my Mum, watching her create holes in her scalp. There are a few shrivels of dried confetti on her dress. When she is nearly bald, I can't look anymore; I have to turn away.

A voice says, *We've all been looking for you.* I spin back. Dad? Mum blurs, quivers, and then she is Philippa. *How could you just disappear like that*, she says. *You're so selfish.* Philippa is smoking a thin black cigarette. When she sucks in the smoke, its tip lights up in a miniature bat's face, red eyes glowing. I sit on the edge of the bed, the nubs of my palms on my eyelids. Philippa gently draws my hands down. Her irises and pupils have swapped their colours, blue discs in the centre rimmed by circles of black. An exhalation of her cigarette smoke takes shape, becomes an ethereal bat that swoops towards me, and I hear her laughter as I duck down. *Ssh,* she reassures me. *Ssh.* Her hands massage mine, taking each of my fingers in turn, until she places a kiss on my palm, her lips so cold it's like holding a snowflake. When she whispers her name, her voice sounds disconnected. The mirror's reflections show me the truth: this is Gina. I don't know if she's under some spell, morphing like a chameleon, or my perception has splintered like a kaleidoscope. A scream is rising in my chest; I can't bear any more of this torture. I try to push her away, but she forces me down onto the bed, whispering no, please don't resist me, you're my hero, I'm your temptress, you're my hero…

viii)

Up on the roof, the cold air blows my mind free of fog. Dad intervened. He stopped the chaos, saved me from Gina's temptation.

"Boy A leaves the bedroom," he says, *"and goes out into the hallway, where he seeks the stairs that lead to the roof."*

Gina folds her arms, shivering in the chill. I keep my distance from her, walking to the edge of the roof, where the thick castellations cut into the sky. I've never liked heights and for a moment the view seesaws in nausea, the trees and the turrets and the gravel driveway. The sun is sinking; a faint moon appearing opposite. Can it really be sunset? The library seems a long time ago, made blurry by the fog, but surely a whole day can't have passed? Perhaps the days are shorter here. I want to be home. I'm tired, so tired of being here. I don't believe that Dad is in this house. I don't believe he's in the woods, waiting for me. Perhaps this place is a kind of psychic skeleton, the remnants of him; he's gone. And Gina – I think she's mad. I don't want to take her back into the world, though I suppose it is my duty. This place has turned her into a spectre.

His voice again.

I look at Gina. Surprise on our faces. We weren't expecting another instruction so soon.

"This is the moment where Boy A meets Boy B."

We look around, seeking *B*, as though his shadowy form might materialise.

"Boy A and Boy B make their way over to the trapdoors."

"Maybe you're supposed to be *Boy B*," I reply. I search Gina's face for recognition, but it remains blank.

We find the trapdoors cut into the far end of the roof. Not just one door, but two. Each has a heavy handle attached to it. Dad's voice startles us again:

"One trapdoor leads back into the haunted Castle. The other will leads back to the real world."

A dramatic pause.

"But only one can return.

"The trapdoors must both be opened at the same time.

"Boy A and Boy B must make a joint decision."

We've been debating for five minutes now, up on the roof, the wind tugging our hair and clothes.

"You didn't find these trapdoors before, when you've been here all these years?"

"No," Gina says. She looks confused. "It's… it must be you, being here, that made them appear."

I enjoy a moment's pride before reality sobers me up. If she's right, and I've created this opportunity, then I ought to behave like a true hero. I should make the sacrifice. Allow her to go. Being told what to do, following *Boy A*'s set path, was riling me but now I feel lost, free will a weight.

I gaze out, beyond the sweep of the gravel driveway to the woods beyond.

"Have you ever got out of the Castle? Did you ever see Dad? I mean, not the omniscient way, but – properly." My voice becomes small; I'm scared she's going to laugh at me.

She touches my arm. "I never met your father as – a human, no. I have reached the woods once or twice, but they fade into white page. I think your Dad didn't imagine anything in this book beyond them." She pauses and a look passes over her face, one I can't quite decipher. "I think you should take the door on the right."

"Okay," I reply, trying to keep my tone casual.

She's lying. I think. She's playing me. She's trying to make me feel like a hero, weaving a costume for me, draping her cloak of flattery around my shoulders.

"I think the door on the right will take you home," she says. "I have a gut feeling, no more than that. We can't be sure. We just have to try. But you – you deserve to be the one to go home. You're young, you have your whole life ahead of you."

"You have a son."

"I… I know." She swallows, tears in her eyes.

"Did you and Dad – did you have an affair?"

She tries to guide me towards the trapdoors. "We should get this over with. You take the right."

"Wait. I want to know – did you and Dad have an affair?"

"No, of course not."

"You're in the paintings, downstairs. Is that because you wanted to get off with him?"

"No. I was his assistant. I liked his books, I admired him, I wanted to do a good job."

"He loved my Mum, you know. He said that other women were coming after him all the time, but he wasn't interested in them because he just loved Mum and me."

"I know that. I saw him how he looked at her. I heard

him say how much he cared about you. I remember that on your tenth birthday he spent the day blowing up balloons for you, twisting them into ghoulish shapes – do you remember that?"

I smile, softening with the memory.

"And I loved my husband and my son," she insists. "I had no interest in your Dad. My Dan – we've known each other since we were kids. We grew up together. He was my best friend and I've never wanted anyone else."

"Okay." I shove my hands in my pockets. "Sorry – I had to ask."

"It's fine. You didn't want to go home with unanswered questions, you wanted resolution. I understand."

"Okay. I guess, then…"

"We'll say goodbye."

I take a step back. "Bye, then."

We take our positions side by side in front of the trapdoors. I follow her suggestion. I take the right; she takes the left. Her expression is that of a martyr. How can *a gut feeling* produce such certainty?

"You have played this game before," I assert.

A pause, followed by a quick denial. She keeps her eyes fixed on the trapdoor. I continue to stare at her, fiercely, until she finally dares to look at me.

"Okay..." her voice is small. "Yes... I have played it. But I'm not lying. The right trapdoor leads to freedom."

"Who did you play it with?"

"Just a character, a ghostly thing, it seemed to be part of the story."

"And you chose the left?"

"Yes. I lost."

How can she imagine that I'd be this stupid? Then she touches her face wearily and I notice her raw, wrecked nails. I remember how desperately she scrabbled at the front door bolt; I think of the lonely scrawl on those papers in the library. I can't blame her for trying to trick me. I'd probably do the same.

So I force a smile at her, and say yes, we'll stick to the plan, and count back from three.

Three...

Two...

My stomach is churning and I have to keep swallowing away the tension in my jaw. I feel as though a part of me is detached from the action, watching myself in horror, observing the ruthlessness of my survival instincts: *Will you really do this? Don't you want to be a hero?* But I do it anyway, even though it sickens me: I push Gina to one side and say I am going down the left trapdoor and she must take the right. Her furious protests confirm that I was correct. She was conning me. My Dad's voice overhead warns us that *we must make a decision,* or risk staying here forever. The rust of the handle scrapes against my palm. Gina reaches for hers, grim-faced, shaking her head.

One.

We lift them in unison.

Each of our trapdoors offers the same view: a set of stone steps that disappear into darkness.

I call out *goodbye* and *sorry,* but she doesn't reply. As I climb down, I tell myself that I'll make it up to her, I'll try to find a way to get her out once I'm home, or else get a message to her husband. I'm doing the right thing. Her husband and her son have each other. My Mum has nobody.

Down, down, down, I go, my steps ringing out, and I think of being home again, of being able to lie in my bed and read Nietzsche, or roam through the fields to the Temptress and sip a pint, or bike with Philippa and kiss her again and do it properly this time, and then there will be uni and my degree and a whole new set of experiences that will make this madness fade into myth, into something I'll probably never believe really happened to me anyway, and I continue down, down, down, until I reach a door, and I push hard to open it and I'm in the grand hallway. Back where I started.

ix)

In the library, at my Dad's desk, I sit down and I read through her papers. Some are stories, some diary entries, some fragments. Over a number of days, I thread them together, forming a story:

Gina met my father at a literary party in 1962. She was a waitress. She served him a glass of champagne and he told her that she was the most beautiful woman in the room. She'd been feeling shabby in her cheap black dress, wealthy people strutting around her. He made her feel human. He told her that he needed a new assistant and she should apply.

The job interview took place in his study. Him behind his desk, her in a rickety wooden chair. During the middle of the interview, my father suddenly asked her to come close to him so that he could examine her fingernails. Each finger was carefully caressed in turn; he concluded that her hands looked fit for a typewriter. He kissed her palm. He told that she must only work for him, that she must type his masterpieces. She reflects with hindsight that this was patronising but at the time, she was thrilled by the flattery. She saw him as a hero. A great man.

She remembers me. I was a boy then and once, when she was in my father's study, working quietly so as not to disturb him whilst he wrote, she saw me on the lawn: I fell off my tricycle and burst into tears. Dad just looked up and stared blankly. She said: "Aren't you going to…?" and he replied, "I'm just in mid-chapter." She faltered, wondered whether to dare venture out and pick me up herself, when she saw my mother appear and hug me tight. Watching us cut her up. She kept picturing scenarios where my mum was out of the picture, where she became my mother.

Then Gina fell pregnant. Her husband didn't suspect a thing. She gave birth to a son. She called him Gabriel, the name of Dad's current protagonist. That's when Dad started to change. He became distant, frosty. He kept telling her that Gabriel was *her* son. He already had a son of his own. Her hours were reduced, her wages. One day she came into work to find a woman sitting at her desk, wearing a pink dress, typing at her typewriter. The woman was called Angela. She looked up and gave Gina a smirk. Dad didn't look up. He just said, "I'll send your final cheque in the post." When she asked why she'd been dismissed, she stroked her belly gently, feeling his baby kick in response. He replied that her work hadn't been up to scratch.

Gina stayed at home and looked after Gabriel whilst her husband tried to find work. She sent my Dad letter after letter: angry, desperate, cajoling, begging. She would never love anyone, she wrote, the way that she loved him. She was trying to be a better person, one who might deserve him. He was her master: she would do whatever she told him. But surely she did not deserve such punishment?

One evening, she turned up at his house, interrupted a family dinner. She demanded royalties, credit for her contribution to his work. He put down his knife and fork and asked her to come into his study. In there, he pulled off the leather glove from her right hand. He said that he could not hire her again unless he examined her fingers, the hands that belonged to him. She remembers a needle that he pulled from a drawer in his desk; a slit in her skin; his voice saying, *I've got a book that's just right for you.* When she woke up, she found herself in the haunted Castle.

But this is a house made for two.

Two stories. Two protagonists, vying. When she arrived, she found a woman here, trapped in a coffin. A previous assistant, one of the early ones. Her name was Martha. They played the game of trapdoors and Martha won, escaped, and Gina replaced her.

(Is this detail real, I wonder. I think I remember one of his assistants going missing; a police interview. But it was so long ago…)

Gina remembers that when Dad was writing a novel, he kept a notebook, where he'd cut and paste deleted scenes, scraps, a sub-plot that wouldn't fit the main, a character whom he wanted to play with later. This Castle, she argues, was the equivalent of that notebook. A place for the untidy, frayed threads of his life; the bits that wouldn't fit into his narrative of a happy, successful family man with a wife and son. And so the Castle became a storeroom crossed with a torture chamber.

I take a candle and I feed the edges of Gina's papers into the flame. A corner licks up, curls into ash – before I throw them down and stamp it out quickly. I put them in a drawer for a day or so, before the masochistic itch comes to reread them, reread them.

I go into the hallway and I shout DAD
DAD
DAD
Until my voice breaks into splinters.

Boy A, Boy B. I play out their stories on alternate days, *Boy A* bold, *Boy B* nervous, one confronting danger, the other running, but Gina was right: their plotlines still include the same clichés and overlap until they reach the same conclusion. Still, I feel the pain of it, that first choice: would it have ended all differently that day if I had chosen *B*, if I had been honest rather than playing a part?

Upstairs on the roof, I go to the trapdoor, the left one, and try to yank it up, whilst Dad's instructions sound over and over. I do this until my palms bleed. But I cannot open it.

I go to the hallway and slice through the cobwebs and I stare at the paintings. I scratch at the woman's face until her paint-skin flakes under my nails, until her face is etched to nothingness, but when I come back the next day the painting is intact.

This is the fifth draft I've written. This one is the longest so far, my first was only 5 pages. I've still missed stuff out like the argument I had with Mum at lunch before I left her behind. Writing in the present this time has made me feel better. Those other drafts in the past tense made me feel as though I was writing my obituary. I'm still here, in the Castle, writing at the oak desk, and Dad's sentinel trees watch me sternly. I've tried to craft my story the way Dad wrote his books. I didn't know how to tell it, so I sat and read his novels for about half an hour before each writing session, until his style seeped into me and flowed through me.

I'm not frightened of this place anymore. The bats, the skeletons, the dogs – they can't raise my heartbeat. It's like being in a doll's house where everything is mechanised. Sometimes I need to wander about, just to hear Dad's voice drily stating choices, no matter how much I hate it, because I need to hear human speech or I think I will go mad, and it's like eating a poison that feeds you and makes you sick all at once.

At night I sleep on the floor in the library. By day I walk around the Castle. Sometimes I even beat the book-odds and make it out to the grounds, but even daylight here is murky and it's forever winter, sunset streaking the sky with a red goodbye around four. I've walked and walked through the woods at the back of the Castle and, just like Gina said, they lead into nothingness, pure white page, oblivion.

Sometimes I feel raw with an anger that overwhelms me and I write out different stories where Gina is the heroine and some horrific revenge falls upon her. Sometimes I just sit and sob, picturing Mum sitting at home, eating by herself, wondering where I am. Or Philippa, no doubt with another guy now, getting drunk with him in the Temptress, giving him kisses and cartwheels. I imagine how the world might be, with Nixon clinging onto power, the Vietnam War trickling to an end, the power cuts getting worse. The world moving on without me. I've contemplated going to the top turret and falling, falling, or else lying down and letting the hounds savage me. But then I picture Mum visiting me in hospital, clutching my limp hand, and I know I have to hold on for her. She sensed this book is dangerous. There is just the slightest chance that she might become my hero.

But if not, if she sent this book to the British Library, then maybe I've been archived in some dark place and I'll never be found. Which means the screaming sessions I attempt every day, where I stand in the Grand Hall and I yell and yell, begging for sound to become word, for word to sear onto page, might never provoke someone to pick up the book. Or: I could be back in Dad's library, wedged between a few books; someone might pull me out one day. But I can't give up. I have to keep trying. I have to keep yelling and pray that someday someone will read me…

Join the Society

The Eden Book Society is an ongoing book subscription brought to you by Dead Ink Books. Each book is written by a different author under a pseudonym and each year we select a different year from the society's history to reproduce. There's even a secret newsletter for subscribers only from our resident archivist digging through the Eden family records.

The 1972 books are written by: Alison Moore; Aliya Whiteley; Jenn Ashworth and Richard V. Hirst; Gary Budden; and Sam Mills.

www.EdenBookSociety.com

The 1972 Subscribers

In 1972 the subscribers to the Eden Book Society were…

Adam Lowe
Adam Rains
Adam Sparshott
Adrienne Ou
Agnes Bookbinder
Aki Schilz
Alan Gregory
Alexandra Dimou
Alice Leuenberger
Alison Moore
Aliya Whiteley
Amanda Faye
Amanda Nixon
Andrew Pattenden
Andy Banks
Andy Haigh
Anna Vaught
Anne Cooper
Anthony Craig Senatore
Ashley Stokes
Audrey Meade
Austin Bowers
Barney Carroll
Becky Lea
Ben Gwalchmai
Ben Nichols
Ben Webster
Benjamin Achrén
Benjamin Myers
Blair Rose
blutac318
Brian Lavelle
C Geoffrey Taylor
C. D. Rose
Catherine Fearns
Catherine Spooner
Cato Vandrare
Chris Adolph and Erika Steiskal
Chris Kerr
Chris Naylor-Ballesteros
Chris Salt
Christopher Ian Smith
Clare Law

Colette
Conor Griffin
Damian Fuller
Dan Coxon
Daniel Ross
Dave Roberts
David Harris
David Hartley
David Hebblethwaite
Debbie Phillips
Dennis Troyer
Derek Devereaux Smith
Edward S Lavery
Elizabeth Nicole Dillon Christjansen
Elizabeth Smith
Eloise Millar
Emily Oram
Eric Damon Walters
Erik Bergstrom
Erin C
Ex Somnia Press
Fat Roland
Françoise Harvey
Gareth E. Rees
Gemma Sharpe
Gia Mancini McCormick
Gina R. Collia
Green Hand Bookshop, Portland, ME
Gregory Martin
Hannah allan
Harry Gallon
Hayley Hart
Heather Askwith
Helen de Búrca
Ian McMillan
Imogen Robertson
Inés G. Labarta
Jack Hook
James Smythe
Jamie Delano
Jamie Lin
Jayne White
Jean Rath
Jen Hinton
Jen Lammey
Jenna H.
Jennifer Bernstein
Jennifer Rainbow
Jim Ryan
Jo Bellamy
John P. Fedele
Jon and Rebecca Cook

Jon Peachey
Joseph Camilleri
Joshua Bartolome
Joshua Cooper
Justine Taylor
Karen Featherstone
Kate Armstrong
Kate Leech
Kathryn Williams
Kelly Hoolihan
Ken Newlands
Kiran Milwood Hargrave
Kirsty Mackay
Laura Carberry
Laura Elliott
Lee Rourke
Livia Llewellyn
Louise Thompson
Lucie McKnight Hardy
Madeleine Anne Pearce
Mairi McKay
Majda Gama
Margot Atwell
Maria Kaffa
Mark Gerrits
Mark John Williamson
Mark Richards
Mark Scholes
Martin van der Grinten
Matt Brandenburg
Matt Neil Hill
Matt Thomas
Matthew Adamson
Matthew Craig
Michael Cieslak
Michael Paley
Mitch Harding
Nancy Johnson
Naomi Booth
Naomi Frisby
Nathan Ballingrud
Nici West
Nick Garrard
Nick Wilson
Nicola Kumar
Nikki Brice
Nina Allan
Owen Clements
Paul Gorman
Paul Hancock
Paul Tremblay
Peter Farr
Peter Haynes
Philip Young

Ray Reigadas
Rhiannon Angharad Grist
Rhodri Viney
Richard Grainger
Richard Kemble
Richard Sheehan
Ricki Schwimmer
Rob Dex
Robb Rauen
Robert P. Goldman
Robin Hargreaves
Robyn Groth
Rodney O'Connor
Rudi Dornemann
Ruth Nassar
S. Kelly
Sanjay Cheriyan Mathew
Sarah R.
Sardonicus
Scarlett Letter
Scarlett Parker
Simon Petherick
Sophie Wright
Spence Fothergill
Stephanie Wasek
Steve Birt
Steven Jasiczek
STORGY Magazine
Taé Tran
Tania
Terra & Bill Jackson
The Contiguous Pashbo
The Paperchain Podcast
Thom Cuell
Thomas Houlton
Tim & Meg
Tim Major
Timothy J. Jarvis
Tom Clarke
Tom Jordan
Tom Ward
Tony Messenger
Tracey Connolly
Tracey Thompson
V Shadow
V. Ganjanakij
Verity Holloway
Vince Haig
Wheeler Pryor
Yvonne Singh
Zoe Mitchell

Also from the Eden Book Society...

Holt House

L. G. Vey

It's a quiet house, sheltered, standing in a mass of tangled old trees called the Holtwood. Raymond watches it. He's been watching it, through a gap in the fence at the bottom of the garden, for weeks. Thinking about the elderly owners, Mr and Mrs Latch, who took him in one night when he was a frightened boy caught up in an emergency. Mr Latch showed him something that was kept in a wardrobe in the spare room. He can't remember what it was. He only knows how sick it made him feel. Raymond watches Holt House. He has to remember what he saw. He has to get inside.

Plunge Hill: A Case Study
J.M. McVulpin

In 1972, during the chaotic days of miners' strikes and the three-day week, Bridget 'Brix' Shipley moves to Plunge Hill to start her new job as a medical secretary at the local hospital.

As she writes to Maurice, her younger brother, sick at home, it becomes clear that not all is well at Plunge Hill. There are frequent power cuts and she has to work by candlelight. While she'd hoped this might inspire some blitz spirit and solidarity between her, the other secretaries and the medical staff, she's increasingly isolated and seemingly ignored by her co-workers.

When originally released in 1972, Plunge Hill pushed the boundaries of the epistolary format within horror. Nearly fifty years on and the novella has lost none of its power to shock the reader with its terrifying portrayal of both the real and imagined goings on at Plunge Hill.

Judderman

D. A. Northwood

London, early-1970s: a city plagued with disappearances, football violence, Republican bombings, blackouts and virulent racism. A new urban myth is taking hold. Among the broken-down estates, crumbling squats and failed projects of a dying metropolis, whispered sightings of a malevolent figure nicknamed the Judderman are spreading. A manifestation of the sick metropolitan psyche, or something else?

Gary Eider's brother loved London, and was terrified by it. And now he's gone; he saw something no one else was willing to see. To find his brother, Gary must descend into the city and its violence, its hate, and its spite. There is something lurking there and it holds the answers to the city.

A Dedicated Friend

Shirley Longford

In 1972 organ donation is in its infancy and Daisy Howard, who is giving a kidney to her aunt, is in the hands of a pioneering surgeon. After the operation, Daisy is desperate to get back to her family, yet the days go by and she remains in the hospital; meanwhile, an old friend keeps visiting with news of home, and Daisy becomes increasingly uneasy.

How much can a friend in need really ask for? And how much can we really forgive them?